Alfred's

INSTRUMENTAL
CD+ INSIDE
PLAY-ALONG

Violin

billboard
GREATEST CHART ALL-STARS
Instrumental Solos

Arranged by Bill Galliford
and Ethan Neuburg

Recordings produced by
Dan Warner, Doug Emery
and Lee Levin

GREATEST CHART ALL-STARS

Top performing songs and artists from the
Billboard Hot 100 and Billboard Hot 200
over the past 50 years

© 2016 Alfred Music
All Rights Reserved. Printed in USA.

ISBN-10: 1-4706-3710-3
ISBN-13: 978-1-4706-3710-1

Alfred

billboard © 2015 Billboard/Prometheus Global Media, LLC All Rights Reserved.

Alfred Cares. Contents printed on environmentally responsible paper.

No part of this book shall be reproduced, arranged, adapted, recorded, publicly performed, stored in a retrieval system,
or transmitted by any means without written permission from the publisher. In order to comply with copyright laws,
please apply for such written permission and/or license by contacting the publisher at alfred.com/permissions.

CONTENTS

CONTENTS

SORRY

Track 2: Demo
Track 3: Play-Along

Words and Music by
JUSTIN TRANTER, JULIA MICHAELS,
JUSTIN BIEBER, SONNY MOORE
and MICHAEL TUCKER

Sorry - 2 - 1

© 2015 WARNER-TAMERLANE PUBLISHING CORP., JUSTIN'S SCHOOL FOR GIRLS and THANKS FOR THE SONGS RICHARD
All Rights on behalf of Itself, JUSTIN'S SCHOOL FOR GIRLS and THANKS FOR THE SONGS RICHARD
Administered by WARNER-TAMERLANE PUBLISHING CORP.
All Rights Reserved

Track 4: Demo
Track 5: Play-Along

FIREWORK

Words and Music by
KATY PERRY, MIKKEL ERIKSEN,
TOR ERIK HERMANSEN, SANDY WILHELM
and ESTER DEAN

Moderate rock (♩ = 126)

Firework - 2 - 1

© 2010 WHEN I'M RICH YOU'LL BE MY B****, EMI APRIL MUSIC PUBLISHING, INC.,
DIPIU SRL (Administered by ULTRA TUNES (ASCAP)) and DAT DAMN DEAN MUSIC
All Rights for WHEN I'M RICH YOU'LL BE MY B**** Administered by WB MUSIC CORP.
All Rights Reserved

STAIRWAY TO HEAVEN

Words and Music by
JIMMY PAGE and ROBERT PLANT

Stairway to Heaven - 2 - 1

© 1972 (Renewed) FLAMES OF ALBION MUSIC, INC.
All Rights Administered by WB MUSIC CORP.
Exclusive Print Rights Administered by ALFRED MUSIC
All Rights Reserved

Track 8: Demo
Track 9: Play-Along

DON'T STOP BELIEVIN'

Words and Music by
JONATHAN CAIN, NEAL SCHON
and STEVE PERRY

Don't Stop Believin' - 2 - 1

© 1981 WEEDHIGH-NIGHTMARE MUSIC and LACEY BOULEVARD MUSIC
All Rights for WEEDHIGH-NIGHTMARE MUSIC Administered by WIXEN MUSIC PUBLISHING INC.
All Rights Reserved

SEE YOU AGAIN

(from *Furious 7*)

Words and Music by
CAMERON THOMAZ, CHARLIE PUTH,
ANDREW CEDAR and JUSTIN FRANKS

Track 10: Demo
Track 11: Play-Along

See You Again - 2 - 1

© 2015 WARNER-TAMERLANE PUBLISHING CORP., WIZ KHALIFA PUBLISHING,
CHARLIE PUTH MUSIC PUBLISHING, ARTIST 101 PUBLISHING GROUP, J FRANKS PUBLISHING,
ANDREW CEDAR PUBLISHING, ARTIST PUBLISHING GROUP WEST, U.P.G. MUSIC PUBLISHING and UNIVERSAL PICTURES MUSIC
All Rights on behalf of itself, WIZ KHALIFA PUBLISHING, CHARLIE PUTH MUSIC PUBLISHING and ARTIST 101 PUBLISHING GROUP
Administered by WARNER-TAMERLANE PUBLISHING CORP.
All Rights for J FRANKS PUBLISHING, ANDREW CEDAR PUBLISHING and ARTIST PUBLISHING GROUP WEST Administered by WB MUSIC CORP.
All Rights for U.P.G. MUSIC PUBLISHING Administered by SONGS OF UNIVERSAL, INC.
All Rights Reserved

Track 12: Demo
Track 13: Play-Along

MR. KNOW IT ALL

Words and Music by
BRETT JAMES, ESTER DEAN,
BRIAN KENNEDY and DANTE JONES

Moderate rock (♩ = 100)

Mr. Know It All - 2 - 1

© 2011 WB MUSIC CORP., EXTERNAL COMBUSTION MUSIC, BRETT JAMES SONGS, SONGS OF UNIVERSAL, INC.,
DAT DAMN DEAN MUSIC, UNIVERSAL MUSIC CORPORATION, B-UNEEK and ALL FOR MELODIE MUSIC
All Rights on behalf of itself, EXTERNAL COMBUSTION MUSIC and BRETT JAMES SONGS Administered by WB MUSIC CORP.
All Rights Reserved

Track 14: Demo
Track 15: Play-Along

HONKY TONK WOMEN

Words and Music by
MICK JAGGER and KEITH RICHARDS

* Percussion intro for accompaniment track.

© 1969 (Renewed) ABKCO MUSIC, INC., 85 Fifth Avenue, New York, NY 10003
All Rights Reserved

HOW DEEP IS YOUR LOVE

Track 16: Demo
Track 17: Play-Along

Words and Music by
BARRY GIBB, MAURICE GIBB
and ROBIN GIBB

© 1977 (Renewed) CROMPTON SONGS LLC and GIBB BROTHERS MUSIC
All Rights For CROMPTON SONGS LLC Administered by WARNER-TAMERLANE PUBLISHING CORP.
All Rights Reserved

THE PRAYER

Words and Music by
CAROLE BAYER SAGER and DAVID FOSTER

The Prayer - 2 - 1

© 1998 WARNER-BARHAM MUSIC LLC (BMI)
All Rights Administered by SONGS OF UNIVERSAL, INC. (BMI)
Exclusive Worldwide Print Rights Administered by ALFRED MUSIC
All Rights Reserved

Track 20: Demo
Track 21: Play-Along

GO YOUR OWN WAY

Words and Music by
LINDSEY BUCKINGHAM

Moderately bright rock (♩ = 136)

© 1976 (Renewed) NOW SOUNDS MUSIC
All Rights Reserved

25 OR 6 TO 4

Words and Music by
ROBERT LAMM

Track 22: Demo
Track 23: Play-Along

Moderately bright rock (♩ = 144)

© 1970 (Renewed) SPIRIT CATALOG HOLDINGS, S.à.r.l. and LAMMINATIONS MUSIC
U.S., UK and Canadian Rights for SPIRIT CATALOGUE HOLDINGS, S.à.r.l. Controlled and Administered by SPIRIT TWO MUSIC, INC. (ASCAP)
Rights for the Rest of World are Controlled and Administered by SPIRIT SERVICES HOLDINGS, S.à.r.l.
on behalf of SPIRIT CATALOGUE HOLDINGS, S.à.r.l.
All Rights Reserved   Used by Permission

ALL ABOUT THAT BASS

Track 24: Demo
Track 25: Play-Along

Words and Music by
MEGHAN TRAINOR and KEVIN KADISH

Moderately bright (♩ = 132)

All About That Bass - 3 - 1

© 2014 YEAR OF THE DOG MUSIC (ASCAP), a division of BIG YELLOW DOG, LLC and OVER-THOUGHT UNDER-APPRECIATED SONGS (ASCAP)
International Copyright Secured   All Rights Reserved   Used by Permission

24

MOONDANCE

Words and Music by
VAN MORRISON

© 1970 (Renewed) WB MUSIC CORP. and CALEDONIA SOUL MUSIC
All Rights Administered by WB MUSIC CORP.
All Rights Reserved

Track 28: Demo
Track 29: Play-Along

UPTOWN FUNK!

Words and Music by
BRUNO MARS, JEFF BHASKER, PHILIP LAWRENCE,
DEVON GALLASPY, MARK RONSON, NICHOLAUS WILLIAMS,
LONNIE SIMMONS, RONNIE WILSON, CHARLES WILSON,
RUDOLPH TAYLOR and ROBERT WILSON

Moderate funk (♩ = 112)

Uptown Funk! - 2 - 1

© 2014 WB MUSIC CORP., THOU ART THE HUNGER, MARS FORCE MUSIC, BMG CHRYSALIS, WAY ABOVE MUSIC,
SONY/ATV SONGS LLC, IMAGEM MUSIC LLC, TIG7 PUBLISHING LLC, TRINLANTA PUBLISHING and MINDER MUSIC
All Rights on behalf of itself and THOU ART THE HUNGER Administered by WB MUSIC CORP.
All Rights Reserved

STYLE

Track 30: Demo
Track 31: Play-Along

Words and Music by
ALI PAYAMI, JOHAN SCHUSTER,
MAX MARTIN and TAYLOR SWIFT

Moderately (♩ = 96)

© 2014 WARNER/CHAPPELL MUSIC SCANDINAVIA AB, WOLF COUSINS, MXM MUSIC AB and TAYLOR SWIFT MUSIC
All Rights in the U.S. and Canada for WARNER/CHAPPELL MUSIC SCANDINAVIA AB and WOLF COUSINS Administered by WB MUSIC CORP.
All Rights for MXM MUSIC AB Administered by KOBALT MUSIC PUBLISHING AMERICA
All Rights for TAYLOR SWIFT MUSIC Administered by SONY/ATV MUSIC PUBLISHING
All Rights Reserved

OPEN ARMS

Words and Music by
JONATHAN CAIN and STEVE PERRY

© 1981 WEEDHIGH-NIGHTMARE MUSIC and LACEY BOULEVARD MUSIC
All Rights for WEEDHIGH-NIGHTMARE MUSIC Administered by WIXEN MUSIC PUBLISHING, INC.
All Rights Reserved

Track 34: Demo
Track 35: Play-Along

HOTEL CALIFORNIA

Words and Music by
DON HENLEY, GLENN FREY
and DON FELDER

Hotel California - 3 - 1

© 1976 (Renewed) CASS COUNTY MUSIC, RED CLOUD MUSIC and FINGERS MUSIC
All Print Rights for CASS COUNTY MUSIC and RED CLOUD MUSIC Administered by WARNER-TAMERLANE PUBLISHING CORP.
All Rights Reserved

(I CAN'T GET NO) SATISFACTION

Track 36: Demo
Track 37: Play-Along

Words and Music by
MICK JAGGER and KEITH RICHARDS

Moderately, driving (♩ = 132)

© 1965 (Renewed) ABKCO MUSIC, INC., 85 Fifth Avenue, New York, NY 10003
All Rights Reserved

I DON'T WANT TO MISS A THING

(from *Armageddon*)

Track 38: Demo
Track 39: Play-Along

Words and Music by
DIANE WARREN

I Don't Want to Miss a Thing - 2 - 1

© 1998 REALSONGS (ASCAP)
All Rights Reserved

DANCING QUEEN

Words and Music by
BENNY ANDERSSON, STIG ANDERSON
and BJORN ULVAEUS

Dancing Queen - 2 - 1

© 1976 (Renewed) POLAR MUSIC AB (Sweden)
All Rights in the U.S. and Canada Administered by EMI GROVE PARK MUSIC, INC. and UNIVERSAL-SONGS OF POLYGRAM INTERNATIONAL, INC.
Exclusive Print Rights for EMI GROVE PARK MUSIC INC. Administered by ALFRED MUSIC
All Rights for UK/Eire Administered by BOCU MUSIC LTD.
All Rights Reserved

Dancing Queen - 2 - 2

Track 42: Demo
Track 43: Play-Along

21 GUNS

Words and Music by
BILLIE JOE, GREEN DAY,
DAVID BOWIE and JOHN PHILLIPS

21 Guns - 2 - 1

© 2009 WB MUSIC CORP., GREEN DAZE MUSIC, UNIVERSAL MUSIC CORPORATION, TINTORETTO MUSIC and RZO MUSIC LTD.
All Rights on behalf of itself and GREEN DAZE MUSIC Administered by WB MUSIC CORP.
[This song contains elements of *"All The Young Dudes"* by David Bowie, © 1972 (Renewed) RZO Music Ltd., Tintoretto Music, Chrysalis Music Ltd. and EMI Music Publishing
and *"San Francisco (Be Sure To Wear Flowers In Your Hair)"* by John Phillips, © 1967 (Renewed) Universal Music Corp.]
All Rights Reserved

Track 44: Demo
Track 45: Play-Along

LIVE AND LET DIE

Words and Music by
PAUL McCARTNEY and
LINDA McCARTNEY

Live and Let Die - 2 - 1

© 1973 (Renewed) UNITED ARTISTS MUSIC LTD. and McCARTNEY MUSIC LTD.
All Rights for UNITED ARTISTS MUSIC LTD. Controlled and Administered by EMI UNART CATALOG INC. (Publishing) and ALFRED MUSIC (Print)
All Rights Reserved

Track 46: Demo
Track 47: Play-Along

NOBODY DOES IT BETTER

(from *The Spy Who Loved Me*)

Music by MARVIN HAMLISCH
Lyrics by CAROLE BAYER SAGER

© 1977 (Renewed) DANJAQ S.A.
All Rights Controlled and Administered by EMI U CATALOG INC./EMI UNART CATALOG INC. (Publishing) and ALFRED MUSIC (Print)
All Rights Reserved

THE GREATEST LOVE OF ALL

Words by
LINDA CREED

Music by
MICHAEL MASSER

© 1977 (Renewed) EMI GOLD HORIZON MUSIC CORP. and EMI GOLDEN TORCH MUSIC CORP.
Exclusive Print Rights Administered by ALFRED MUSIC
All Rights Reserved

Track 50: Demo
Track 51: Play-Along

LOVE ME LIKE YOU DO

Words and Music by
ALI PAYAMI, ILYA, TOVE LO,
MAX MARTIN and SAVAN KOTECHA

Moderately slow (♩ = 96)

Love Me Like You Do - 2 - 1

© 2015 WARNER/CHAPPELL MUSIC SCANDINAVIA AB, WOLF COUSINS, MXM MUSIC AB and UNIVERSAL PICTURES MUSIC
All Rights in the U.S. and Canada for WARNER/CHAPPELL MUSIC SCANDINAVIA AB and WOLF COUSINS Administered by WB MUSIC CORP.
All Rights Reserved

Love Me Like You Do - 2 - 2

JUST THE WAY YOU ARE (AMAZING)

Track 52: Demo
Track 53: Play-Along

Words and Music by
KHALIL WALTON, PETER HERNANDEZ,
PHILIP LAWRENCE, ARI LEVINE
and KHARI CAIN

Moderately (♩ = 112)

Just the Way You Are (Amazing) - 2 - 1

© 2010 WB MUSIC CORP., UPPER DEC, ROC NATION MUSIC, MUSIC FAMAMANEM, NORTHSIDE INDEPENDENT MUSIC PUBLISHING LLC,
ROUND HILL SONGS, BUGHOUSE, MARS FORCE MUSIC, UNIVERSAL MUSIC CORP. and DRY RAIN ENTERTAINMENT
All Rights on behalf of itself, UPPER DEC, ROC NATION MUSIC and MUSIC FAMAMANEM Administered by WB MUSIC CORP.
All Rights for BUGHOUSE and MARS FORCE MUSIC Administered by BUG MUSIC/BMG RIGHTS MANAGEMENT (US) LLC
All Rights on behalf of itself and DRY RAIN ENTERTAINMENT Controlled and Administered by UNIVERSAL MUSIC CORP.
All Rights Reserved

Just the Way You Are (Amazing) - 2 - 2

DESPERADO

Words and Music by
DON HENLEY and GLENN FREY

Desperado - 2 - 1

© 1973 (Renewed) CASS COUNTY MUSIC and RED CLOUD MUSIC
All Print Rights Administered by WARNER-TAMERLANE PUBLISHING CORP.
All Rights Reserved

ROAR

Track 56: Demo
Track 57: Play-Along

Words and Music by
KATY PERRY, LUKASZ GOTTWALD,
MAX MARTIN, BONNIE McKEE
and HENRY WALTER

Moderate pop rock (♩ = 90)

© 2013 WB MUSIC CORP., WHEN I'M RICH YOU'LL BE MY B****, KASZ MONEY PUBLISHING,
MARATONE AB, BONNIE MCKEE MUSIC and PRESCRIPTION SONGS, LLC
All Rights on behalf of itself and WHEN I'M RICH YOU'LL BE MY B**** Administered by WB MUSIC CORP.
All Rights Reserved

Track 58: Demo
Track 59: Play-Along

YOU RAISE ME UP

Words and Music by
ROLF LOVLAND and
BRENDAN GRAHAM

Slowly (♩ = 60)

© 2002 UNIVERSAL MUSIC PUBLISHING, a Division of UNIVERSAL MUSIC AS and PEERMUSIC (Ireland) LIMITED
Exclusive Worldwide Print Rights for ROLF LØVLAND Administered by ALFRED MUSIC
All Rights Reserved

SHUT UP AND DANCE

Track 60: Demo
Track 61: Play-Along

Words and Music by
RYAN McMAHON, BENJAMIN BERGER,
NICHOLAS PETRICCA, SEAN WAUGAMAN,
KEVIN RAY and ELI MAIMAN

Moderately bright pop rock (♩ = 129)

Shut Up and Dance - 2 - 1

© 2014 WB MUSIC CORP., RYAN MCMAHON PUBLISHING, BENJAMIN BERGER PUBLISHING,
NICHOLASNICHOLAS MUSIC, TREAT ME BETTER TINA, ANNA SUN MUSIC and VERB TO BE MUSIC
All Rights on behalf of Itself and RYAN MCMAHON PUBLISHING and BENJAMIN BERGER PUBLISHING Administered by WB MUSIC CORP.
All Rights Reserved

Track 62: Demo
Track 63: Play-Along

CAN'T FEEL MY FACE

Words and Music by
ALI PAYAMI, SAVAN KOTECHA,
MAX MARTIN, ABEL TESFAYE
and PETER SVENSSON

Can't Feel My Face - 2 - 1

© 2015 WOLF COUSINS, WARNER/CHAPPELL MUSIC SCANDINAVIA AB, SONGS MUSIC PUBLISHING and MXM
All Rights in the U.S. and Canada for WOLF COUSINS and WARNER/CHAPPELL MUSIC SCANDINAVIA AB Administered by WB MUSIC CORP.
All Rights Reserved

Track 64: Demo
Track 65: Play-Along

CAKE BY THE OCEAN

Words and Music by
JUSTIN TRANTER, ROBIN FREDRIKSSON,
MATTIAS LARSSON and JOE JONAS

Driving dance beat (♩ = 120)

Cake by the Ocean - 2 - 1

© 2015 WARNER-TAMERLANE PUBLISHING CORP., JUSTIN'S SCHOOL FOR GIRLS, WOLF COUSINS,
WARNER/CHAPPELL MUSIC SCANDINAVIA AB, MA-JAY PUBLISHING and SONGS OF UNIVERSAL, INC.
All Rights on behalf of itself and JUSTIN'S SCHOOL FOR GIRLS Administered by WARNER-TAMERLANE PUBLISHING CORP.
All Rights in the U.S. and Canada for WOLF COUSINS, WARNER/CHAPPELL MUSIC SCANDINAVIA AB and MA-JAY PUBLISHING
Administered by WB MUSIC CORP.
All Rights Reserved

Cake by the Ocean - 2 - 2

Track 66: Demo
Track 67: Play-Along

LIKE I'M GONNA LOSE YOU

Words and Music by
JUSTIN WEAVER, CAITLYN SMITH
and MEGHAN TRAINOR

Like I'm Gonna Lose You - 2 - 1

© 2014 WB MUSIC CORP., MUSIC OF THE CORN, YEAR OF THE DOG MUSIC (ASCAP),
a division of BIG YELLOW DOG MUSIC, LLC and MUSIC OF STAGE THREE
All Rights on behalf of itself and MUSIC OF THE CORN Administered by WB MUSIC CORP.
All Rights Reserved